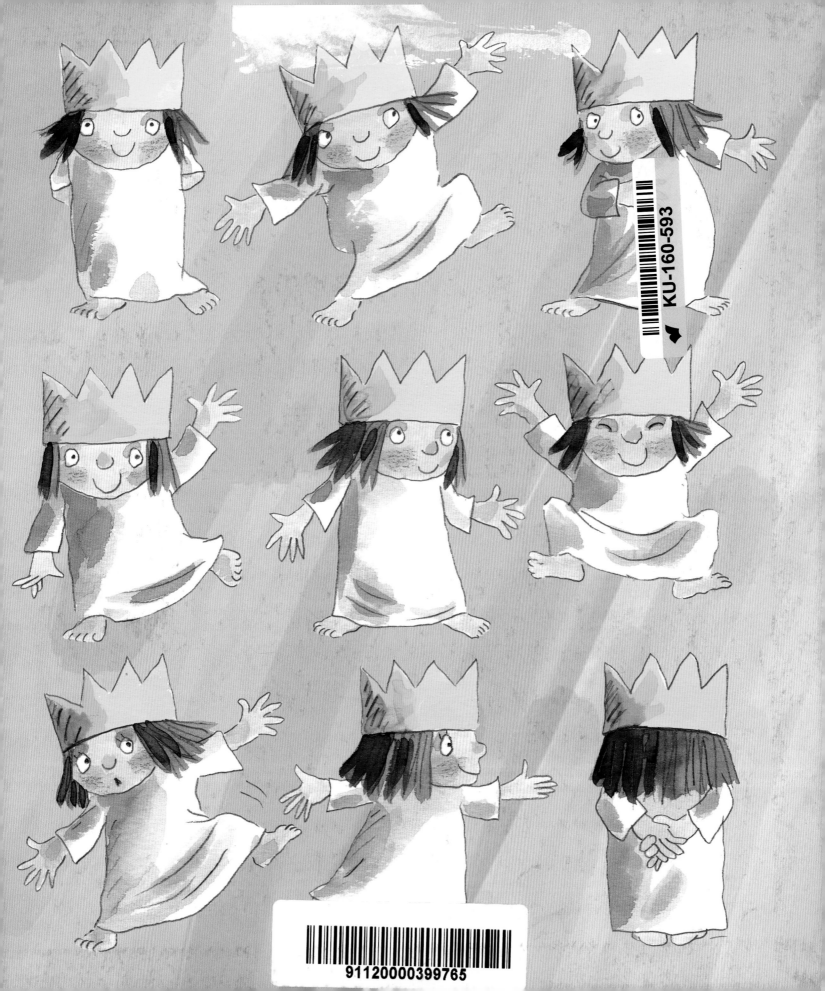

To Aric, Ted and Nell

First published in Great Britain in 2019 by Andersen Press Ltd.,
20 Vauxhall Bridge Road, London SW1V 2SA.
Copyright © Tony Ross, 2019
The right of Tony Ross to be identified as the author and illustrator of this work
has been asserted by him in accordance with the Copyright, Designs and Patents Act, 1988.
All rights reserved. Colour separated in Switzerland by Photolitho AG, Zürich.
Printed and bound in Malaysia.

1   3   5   7   9   10   8   6   4   2

British Library Cataloguing in Publication Data available.

ISBN 978 1 78344 784 8

Little Princess

I Want a Bunny!

Tony Ross

Andersen Press

Once a year, the Little Princess visited her awful friend Petronella.
Petronella was awful because she had all the things the
Little Princess wanted.

Petronella had the fluffiest, cutest, brownest bunny rabbit ever.
She called it Chocky. The Little Princess had *always* wanted a pet,
especially a pet just like that.

"I WANT A BUNNY!" she squealed, over and over again.

"Bunnies are very nice," said the Queen, "but you must remember, YOU would have to clean its cage and its bottom, and feed it every day."

The Gardener overheard the Little Princess and he gave her a less troublesome pet. A stick insect. "His name is Sticky," said the Gardener, "and he lives in trees."

The Little Princess put Sticky in a tree, but she couldn't find him again.

The Admiral gave the Little Princess a goldfish in a bowl.
The Little Princess named her new pet Goldy, and watched it
swim round and round and round and round and round and round.

It was so BORING! To give her pet a bit more fun, she let it swim around in the palace lake, but it swam away and couldn't be found again.

The Cook had a good idea. "Why don't you look after the kitchen cat?" he said. But the cat didn't like being brushed and dressed up, so she scratched off her bow and went to hide in the kitchen.

The Little Princess began to feel that she wasn't very good at having a pet. "Why are you looking so glum?" asked the Queen. "Because all I really want is a bunny!" sniffed the Little Princess.

"Very well," said the Queen, "but you must remember to look after it properly."
"I WILL, I WILL. I WILL, I WILL!" said the Little Princess.

At the pet shop, they bought the cutest, fluffiest, whitest bunny ever. "I'll call it CHALKY!" said the Little Princess.

At first, she looked after Chalky very well: hugging him, cleaning him, feeding him, then hugging him again. "I'll ask Petronella over to see the best bunny in the world," she thought, picking up the phone.

When Petronella arrived at the palace, she was riding her brand new pony. The two girls joggled around the field, Petronella driving, and the Little Princess hanging on behind.

Chalky sat alone and forgotten in his royal hutch.

"I WANT A PONY!" shouted the Little Princess.

"But you've only just got a bunny!" said the Queen.
"Oh yes," said the Little Princess, rushing over to the royal hutch
to see her bunny.

"YEEEEEEK!" squealed the Little Princess, "I've lost my bunny!"
Chalky had nibbled a hole in the wall of his hutch and escaped.

The Little Princess was very sad. The King lifted
his daughter up and kissed her on the nose.

"Don't be sad," he whispered, "Chalky will be very happy now.
He will be hopping free in the forest, and when he is hungry
he will hop back here and eat the Gardener's carrots."

The Little Princess wiped away her tears then she smiled her biggest smile. The King presented her with a new pet. A hobby horse.

"There," said the King, "the perfect pet. You can brush it, you can feed it and you can ride it. What you can't do is LOSE it!"

That is of course, until the General borrowed it
to lead his soldiers…

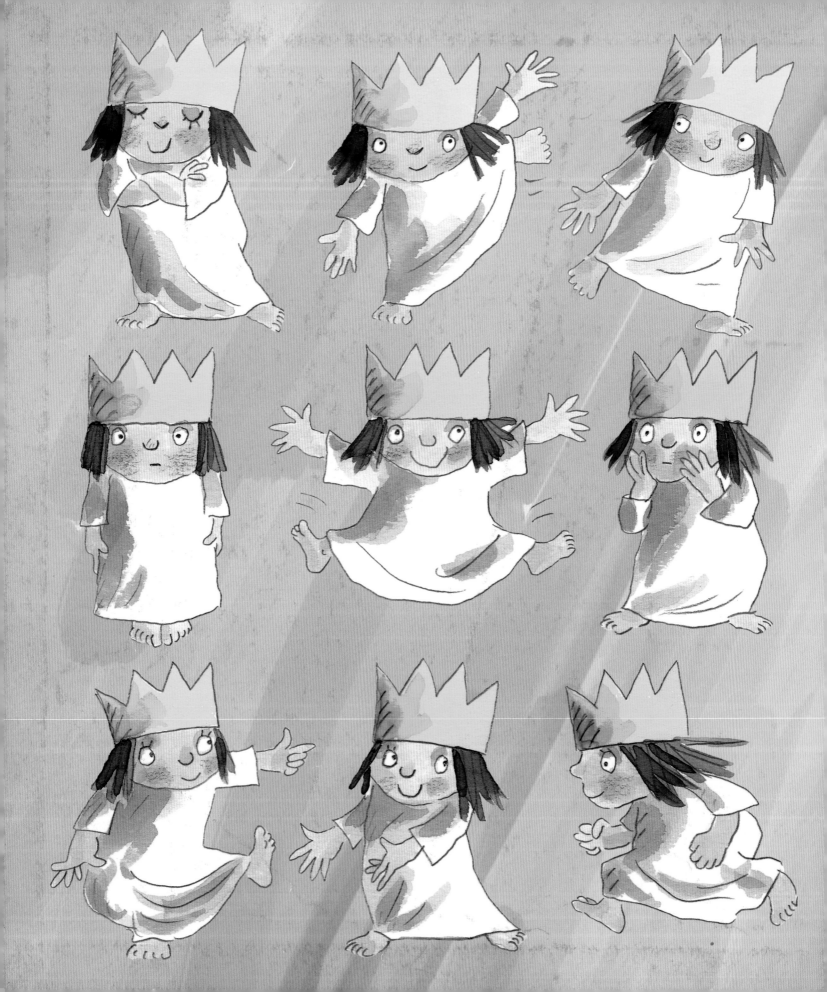